Illustrations by Isabel Muñoz.

Written by Jane Kent.

Designed by Nick Ackland.

WHITE STAR KIDS

White Star Kids® is a registered trademark property of White Star s.r.l.

© 2019 White Star s.r.l.
Piazzale Luigi Cadorna, 6
20123 Milan, Italy
www.whitestar.it

Produced by i am a bookworm.

ISBN 978-88-544-1360-3
1 2 3 4 5 6   23 22 21 20 19

Printed in Turkey

The life of
Frida
Kahlo

WS Kids
WHITE STAR KIDS

I am Frida Kahlo, a Mexican artist famed for both the vibrant colors in my paintings and my colorful life. With my striking face, I was the queen of the self-portrait long before the photo selfies of today.

Join me on my incredible journey from unknown artist to feminist role model whose work now sells for millions.

My full name is Magdalena Carmen Frida Kahlo y Calderón and I was born in Coyoacán, on the outskirts of Mexico City. My date of birth was 6th July 1907, but I would later claim that I came into the world in 1910, to coincide with the beginning of the Mexican Revolution.

Matilde

Wilhelm

Matilde

Adriana

Cristina

Frida

My father, Wilhelm, was a German photographer. He immigrated to Mexico when he was young and later he met and married my mother, Matilde. They had two daughters, Matilde and Adriana, before me and another daughter, Cristina, after me. We all lived together at La Casa Azul, the Blue House.

When I was six years old, I became seriously ill with polio. I wasn't able to leave my bed for nine months and when I finally did walk again, it was with a limp because the disease had permanently damaged my right leg. From then on, it remained shorter than the other leg.

I had been kept in isolation during my recovery and was very lonely, so to aid my recovery my father encouraged me to play football, go swimming and even to wrestle.

In 1922, I was one of the first 35 girls admitted to the renowned National Preparatory School. I was academically gifted, studying medicine, botany and social sciences. I also joined the Young Communist League and the Mexican Communist Party, choosing to socialize with a group of students who were intellectually and politically like-minded.

During that time, I became very interested in Mexican culture. It was the start of a life-long fascination with the Mexican side of my heritage, and I began to experiment with the traditional clothes and jewelry in bold patterns and bright colors which would later become my trademark look.

When I was 18, my first boyfriend, Alejandro Gómez Arias, and I were involved in a terrible traffic accident. On 17th September 1925 the bus we were traveling in hit a tram. Thankfully Alejandro had only minor wounds, but I suffered serious injuries. A handrail pierced my hip and I broke many bones, including my spine, collarbone and pelvis. I spent several months in the Red Cross Hospital in Mexico City, before returning home to continue my recovery there. In the years that followed,
I had around 30 operations and lived
with constant, chronic pain.

While I was confined to my bed in the months after the accident, to take my mind off my situation and relieve my boredom, I began to paint. First I experimented with watercolors and then I moved onto oil. There weren't many objects in my room, but there was a mirror and so I became my primary subject. My first self-portrait was finished in September 1926. I named it "Self-Portrait in a Velvet Dress" and I gifted it to Alejandro, though we were no longer a couple.

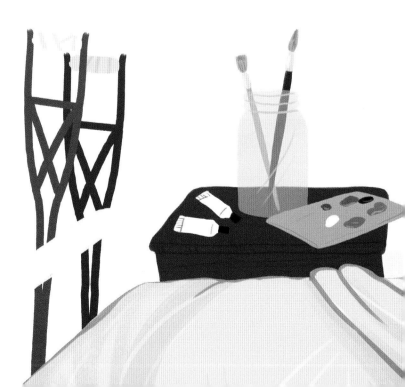

By 1929 I had recovered enough to marry a famous Mexican muralist and fellow Communist called Diego Rivera. We first met in 1922 when he worked on a project at my high school. I had watched in the lecture hall as he painted a huge mural called "The Creation" and was fascinated by him.

When I met him again in 1928 we began a relationship, and the following year I became his wife. We shared political views and we supported and encouraged each other's artistic work, but there was also much we disagreed on. Our marriage was always fiery.

Diego received commissions from all over the world and I often traveled with him. In 1930 we lived in San Francisco, California, and it was there the following year that I painted a wedding portrait called "Frieda and Diego Rivera". I showed it at the Sixth Annual Exhibition of the San Francisco Society of Women Artists.

We moved to New York City in 1933, where Diego was commissioned by Nelson Rockefeller to create a mural for the RCA Building at Rockefeller Center. The mural was called "Man at the Crossroads" and among its hundreds of characters, Diego included a portrait of Communist leader, Vladimir Lenin. Rockefeller was furious and put a stop to the project, then had it painted over. Diego was most unhappy and a few months after this incident, we returned to Mexico, where we hosted the exiled Soviet Communists Leon and Natalia Trotsky in 1937.

I had an exhibition at a New York City gallery in 1938. It was my first solo show and to my delight, I sold about half of the 25 paintings that were on display. This led to a commission from Clare Boothe Luce, the editor of famous fashion magazine "Vanity Fair."

I became good friends with André Breton that same year. He was a leading figure in the Surrealism artistic and literary movement. Although André considered my work to be Surrealist, I disagreed. I painted my reality! However, I did submit two of my paintings to be displayed at the "International Exhibition of Surrealism" in 1940 at the Galeria de Arte Mexicano.

In 1939, I went to live in Paris and displayed my work in the Colle Gallery. The "Mexique" exhibition included a self-portrait with a bright border of birds and flowers called "The Frame". This painting was bought by the Louvre and was the first work by a 20th century Mexican artist to be purchased by the famed art museum.

When I returned home to Mexico, Diego and I divorced. I expressed my feelings in a painting called "The Two Fridas". It showed two versions of me, sitting side by side. One Frida wears white and has a damaged heart, while the other Frida wears bold colors and has an undamaged heart. They represent feeling "unloved" and "loved". However, we found we couldn't stay apart and so the following year, in 1940, I remarried Diego.

By 1941 my work was growing in popularity and had been included in several exhibitions. The Mexican government commissioned me to paint portraits of five important Mexican women. It was extremely exciting, but unfortunately I was unable to complete the project. My beloved father died that year and the health problems I had suffered from for most of my life began to get worse.

I had to have several operations on my spine and in 1944 I painted "The Broken Column" to express how I was feeling. It is a self-portrait, showing me split down the middle with a cracked and broken stone column in place of my spine. There are lots of nails piercing my skin, to represent the constant pain I was in.

My health issues continued and in 1950 I got gangrene in my right foot, which meant spending nine months in the hospital and having several more operations. Although I had limited mobility, I kept on painting and did my best to support political causes that were close to my heart.

1953 was a mixed year for me. In April I was honored to receive my first solo exhibition in my home country of Mexico. I was determined to be there for the opening night despite being bedridden, so I arrived in an ambulance and spent the evening talking with guests from a bed that had been set up in the gallery. Then in August, I had to have part of my right leg removed in order to stop the gangrene from spreading. I chose to wear an ornate red boot on my prosthetic leg.

Throughout the first half of 1954 I was in and out of hospital with various ailments, including bronchial pneumonia. But I would not let my poor health stop my political work, even gathering the strength to join a street demonstration against North-American intervention in Guatemala, which took place in July. It was to be my last public appearance.

On my 47th birthday, I dressed in full costume, did my make-up and put flowers in my hair. I was then carried downstairs to meet my guests. By the evening I was very tired, so I simply asked my guests to join me in my room and continued to chat with them from my bed.

One week after my birthday, I passed away on 13th July, 1954. Many, many people came to my beloved Blue House, where I'd spent my last night, to pay their respects and four years later it was turned into the Museo Frida Kahlo, a house museum. My husband Diego gave it to the Mexican people.

When the feminist movement began in the 1970s, there was renewed interest in my work and I became an icon of female creativity. In the years since my death, several books have been written about me and there is even a film based on my life, made in 2002.

I hope that two essential lessons can be learned from looking back at my life. Firstly, remember that whatever the world throws at you, you can handle it.

Don't let physical pain or disability hold you back or stop you from achieving your dreams. Secondly, it is important to know yourself, so take the time to explore what makes you happy.

Kahlo studied at the National Preparatory School. While there, she became interested in Communism and first met muralist Diego Rivera.

Kahlo was born in Coyoacán, Mexico City, on 6th July.

Kahlo painted "Self-Portrait in a Velvet Dress" during her recovery.

1907 **1922** **1926**

1913 **1925**

A serious traffic accident left Kahlo with a broken spine and put her in hospital for many months.

She suffered from polio at age six and was left with a damaged right leg.

Kahlo and Diego married.

"Frieda and Diego Rivera", a wedding portrait painted by Kahlo, was shown at the Sixth Annual Exhibition of the San Francisco Society of Women Artists.

1929

1931

1928

1930

1933

The newlyweds moved to San Francisco.

Frida began a relationship with Diego Rivera, a fellow Communist.

The couple moved to New York, where Diego had been commissioned to create a mural at Rockefeller Center.

Exiled Soviet Communists Leon and Natalia Trotsky stayed with Kahlo and Diego in Mexico.

Kahlo received a commission from the Mexican government but the project went unfinished due to her ill health and the death of her father.

Kahlo moved to Paris and held her "Mexique" exhibition at the Colle Gallery. She divorced Diego.

1937

1939

1941

1938

1940

Kahlo had her first solo show at a City gallery and she sold lots of paintings. She also met Surrealist artist André Breton.

She displayed two paintings in the "International Exhibition of Surrealism" at the Galeria de Arte Mexicano. Kahlo and Diego remarried.

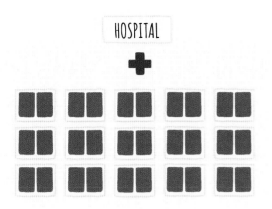

HOSPITAL

Kahlo spent months in hospital after developing gangrene in her right foot.

Kahlo caught bronchial pneumonia and was in and out of hospital for weeks. Her last public appearance was at a political street demonstration.

1950

1954

1944

1953

1954

After undergoing several operations on her spine, Kahlo painted "The Broken Column".

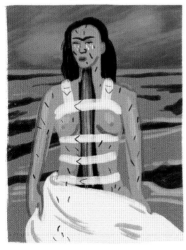

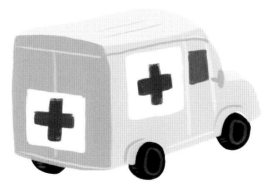

Kahlo passed away on 13th July.

FRIDA KAHLO

She arrived by ambulance to her first solo exhibition in Mexico. Kahlo later had part of her right leg removed and wore a prosthetic leg.

QUESTIONS

Q1. What was the Kahlo's family house called?

Q2. In what year did Frida pretend she was born and why?

Q3. How old was Frida when she contracted polio?

Q4. Frida was one of the first 35 girls admitted to which renowned school?

Q5. Which political movement did Frida become interested in?

Q6. In what year did Frida first marry Mexican muralist Diego Rivera?

Q7. Which exiled Communists did Frida and Diego help in 1937?

Q8. What art style did André Breton consider Frida's work to be?

Q9. What is the title of the 1944 painting that expresses Frida's feelings about her spine operations?

Q10. Frida passed away one week after which birthday?

ANSWERS

A1. La Casa Azul, the Blue House.

A2. 1910, because that was when the Mexican Revolution began.

A3. Six years old.

A4. The National Preparatory School.

A5. Communism.

A6. 1929.

A7. Leon and Natalia Trotsky.

A8. Surrealist.

A9. "The Broken Column".

A10. Her 47th birthday.